# The GHOST in Tent 19

By Jim and Jane O'Connor

Illustrated by Charles Robinson

A STEPPING STONE BOOK

Random House New York

 Published in the United States by Random House, Inc., New York, and simultaneously in Canada by Random House of Canada Limited, Toronto.

*Library of Congress Cataloging-in-Publication Data:*
O'Connor, Jim. The ghost in tent 19. (A Stepping stone book) SUMMARY: A mysterious ghost leads the four boys of tent 19 on the trail of buried pirate treasure. [1. Ghosts—Fiction. 2. Buried treasure—Fiction. 3. Camps—Fiction] I. O'Connor, Jane. II. Robinson, Charles, 1931– ill. III. Title. IV. Title: Ghost in tent nineteen. PZ7.02223Gh 1988 [Fic] 87-28372
ISBN: 0-394-89800-1 (pbk.); 0-394-99800-6 (lib. bdg.)

Manufactured in the United States of America 2 3 4 5 6 7 8 9 0

*For Robby and Teddy*

PINES

# 1.

Everybody always said that Camp Tall Pines was haunted. But nobody really believed it. It was just a story, a good story to tell around a campfire. And that was what our counselor, Ivan, was doing right now on our first camp-out.

"And so beware," Ivan whispered. The fire cast a spooky glow on his round, chubby face. "Beware of the full moon. For that is when a strange mist floats over our tent . . . tent nineteen. Is it fog? No! For if you look closely, you will see a face in the mist. And if you listen closely, you will hear it moan. *Ah-ooh! Ah-ooh!*"

Ivan waggled his stubby fingers at us. Then he let out another big *ah-oooooh!*

My best friend, Jed, rolled his eyes at me. We both think Ivan is kind of a nerd. He really goes overboard with all this corny camp stuff.

"So who is this ghost anyway?" I asked. I tried to sound sarcastic. But the truth is, I don't like mysteries. I don't like stuff you can't explain.

Ivan rubbed the scraggly beard he was trying to grow. "Beats me, Danny," he said, mopping his face with the end of his T-shirt. Nights in Maine were supposed to be cool. But this one sure wasn't.

"It's probably the ghost of some poor kid who died from that poison they call food." That was Hal. Hal wears glasses and is on the small side—except for his mouth. That's big. He hates camp. And he lets everybody know it.

"Maybe it's the ghost of Captain Bloodworth," said Arthur. "He was a famous pirate. And he's supposed to have buried a lot of treasure along the coast of Maine."

"No kidding!" Jed sat up. Jed is a big, slow

sandy-haired kid. Just about the only thing that gets him excited is money.

Arthur nodded. Arthur looks kind of like Alfred E. Neuman. But between those jug ears is one awesome brain. "They say Captain Blood—that's what he was called—always buried a dead guy with the treasure chest. To keep watch."

"Speaking of dead," Ivan said, "that is how you will feel tomorrow if you don't get to sleep." He leaned over and threw dirt on the fire.

We all groaned. No one wanted to get into a sleeping bag on such a warm night. So we took as long as possible getting into our pj's. But after a while Ivan had had enough. "Listen. I want you in those sleeping bags now. Or my middle name isn't—"

"Martin," I said under my breath.

Ivan's head jerked toward me. "How did you know that?"

"Um . . . I saw a tag on your suitcase." I came up with that one fast. But it was a lie.

You see, I am an average kid. Not skinny. Not fat. Brown hair and eyes. The kind of kid you run into all the time. The only thing is, I get strange feelings sometimes. For instance, I knew Arthur was born on July 4 before he ever told me. I try not to think about this too much. Like I said, I don't like stuff you can't explain.

In a little while Ivan was asleep. I could tell by the snoring. Ivan snores so loud, trees seem to shake. I was pretty beat too. We had hiked a long way from camp today. But I couldn't sleep. Shreds of clouds sailed across the sky. As I watched them, the clouds seemed to change shape. They turned into ghostly faces with empty holes for eyes.

"Are you asleep, Danny?" Jed poked me in my side.

"Yes, I am," I hissed.

"Come on. You are not."

"Of course I'm not asleep," I whispered. "I just answered you."

Hal groped for his glasses. "I'm awake too," he said in a low voice. "Boy, is it hot. Even our tent would be cooler than here. Too bad camp is so far away."

"It's not," Arthur rolled over and whispered to us. "All Ivan did was walk us in a big circle. If

we wanted, we could be back at camp in fifteen minutes."

Suddenly that didn't seem like a bad idea.

"Ivan will kill us," Hal said softly.

"Let's worry about that tomorrow," Jed whispered back.

I started laughing. The idea seemed better and better. I could just see our fearless leader, Ivan, waking up alone in the middle of the field. He'd freak out! Jed clamped his hand over my mouth so I wouldn't wake up Ivan. Then quickly and quietly we packed our stuff. Ivan never moved.

As soon as we had our sneakers on, we started through the woods. Arthur led the way, since he knew the shortcut. Jed huffed and puffed behind us.

I am a city kid and, let me tell you, there is nothing blacker than a country night. Even with our flashlights we kept tripping over plants and tree roots. But sure enough, in fifteen minutes we reached camp and walked through the entrance gate.

All the tents at Tall Pines look the same.

They're all dark green and set up on platforms. But you can't miss our tent. Tent 19. It's the very first one you come to. It sits right between two big pine-tree stumps. From our tent you can see all the other tents down the hill. At the very bottom lies the bay. That's where we swim and go sailing.

We were almost at our tent when Jed grabbed my arm.

"Look!" he said.

A strange white glow was coming from inside our tent. It didn't look like the glow of a flashlight. It was much paler.

"Someone's in there!" Arthur said.

Very quietly we crept up a little closer. There *was* someone inside. But it was hard to see who it was through the strange, foggy light. I was beginning to get the creeps.

"I bet some kid is trying to short-sheet our beds," Jed whispered.

I wasn't so sure. But when Hal said, "Let's run in and scare him," I went along with the others. We ran up the steps and burst through the door of the tent. Hal snapped on the light.

"Got you!" Hal shouted.

But no one was there. The tent was absolutely empty.

"Where did he go?" Jed, Hal, and Arthur said at the same time. They started looking under the beds and inside the cubbyholes. I just stood there, rubbing my arms to keep warm.

"What's the matter with you?" asked Arthur.

"Don't you feel the chill?" I asked. "I'm freezing."

"Come on. How can you be cold?" asked Arthur. "It's ninety degrees out."

"I don't know," I said, my teeth chattering. "But I am. . . . I've felt this way before."

"Sure," said Hal. "When you were getting the flu, right?"

"No," I said slowly. "It happens sometimes when I pass a graveyard."

Jed's eyes bugged out. He is the only one I have ever told about my strange feelings. But Arthur had a good laugh.

"Cut it out, Danny," said Arthur. "Next you'll tell me that the ghost of Camp Tall Pines was in here. It was just some kid. That's all. I don't know how he got out of here. But he did."

I kept quiet. They could believe what they wanted. And maybe they were right.

By the time I crawled into bed, the chill was fading away. Still, I pulled my dad's old army blanket over me to keep warm.

I looked over at the big lump in the next cot.

"Night, buddy," I said to Jed. I was glad he was there.

"Boy, I wish I could see Ivan's face in the morning." Jed laughed softly. "The joke is sure on him!"

I forced a laugh too. But I wasn't really in a laughing mood. And I wasn't so sure anymore that the story of the ghost was just a story.

# 2.

Jed was wrong. The joke was not on Ivan. The joke was on us. The next morning we all woke up with poison ivy.

"Great shortcut, Arthur," said Hal. "You must have taken us right through a patch of poison ivy."

"Serves you right."

Ivan—all five feet four inches of him—was standing at the door of the tent. He looked mad. Very mad. "Why did you guys pull a stunt like

that?" he demanded. "I'm responsible for you. What if somebody got hurt? What if Cubby found out? I'd get fired."

Cubby owns Tall Pines. With a name like Cubby, you'd think he'd be a friendly, easygoing kind of guy. But he isn't. Running a camp is strictly business for him.

"Gosh, Ivan," I said. "It was just a joke. We didn't want you to get into trouble. Honest."

Ivan shook his head and rubbed his little beard. "Come on. I'd better get you to the nurse fast. You all look terrible."

I didn't want to go near a mirror. I itched like crazy. And if I looked as bad as everyone else, I wasn't a pretty sight. Jed's face was so puffy, he looked like Porky Pig.

The camp nurse gasped when she saw us.

"It happened on a camp-out" was all Ivan told her. Ivan may act a little nerdy, but he is an okay guy.

After Ivan left, the nurse led each of us to a cot. She coated us with thick, pink lotion and gave us some Jell-O. No matter what's wrong with you, you get Jell-O at the infirmary.

The day really dragged.

On the wall of the infirmary was an old map of Tall Pines. It showed the bay, the dock, and lots of little squares for the tents. At the top of the hill was the little square for tent 19, with small circles on either side for the tree stumps. The map also showed the road that led out to the main highway.

Hal found a pencil and paper and, squinting through his glasses, started drawing a map of his own.

"What are you doing that for?" I asked as I took a Monopoly set down from the shelf.

"This is so I can run away," Hal said in a low voice. "I'm through with this dump. I'm getting out. Soon."

"Right, Hal," I said. Hal talked big, but he'd never have the guts to run away.

I tried to get Jed to play Monopoly. But he was deep in a book on pirates that he'd found. "Maybe there's stuff in here on Captain Blood's treasure," he said.

So that left only Arthur. Arthur always beats me. And sure enough, an hour later he had hotels up all over the place. I was in jail for the third time.

"Guys, listen to this!" Jed cried suddenly. He began to read aloud from his book. " 'Captain Blood was as scary as his name. He stood seven feet tall. He was missing an ear. And he had a long black bread.' "

"You mean beard," I said. Jed is not the hottest reader.

"Oh, right. Beard." Jed went on, " 'He only looted other pirate ships. It is said he stole more gold than any other pirate. And none of it has ever been found. He died in 1717 when his ship sank in a storm.' " Jed laid the book on his big belly. There was a faraway look in his eyes. "Would it ever be cool to find treasure."

"Fat chance," Hal said. He was just finishing his map. "Real kids never find treasure. That only happens in books."

The nurse let us out for dinner. Before we left, she put more pink stuff on us and told us to stay out of the water.

In the mess hall kids took one look at us and started covering their eyes and pretending to throw up. We knew we looked pretty awful, but we tried to act cool about it. We lurched around

like Frankenstein. "We are the living dead," I moaned. "And we are coming to get you!"

The littlest kids screamed and dove under the long picnic-type tables until Cubby gave a blast on his whistle and restored order in the mess hall.

It was still super hot out, and the one fan in the mess hall was broken. In the middle of dinner Cubby blew his whistle again.

"Because of the heat," Cubby announced, "we will have free swim tonight."

Everybody in camp cheered and banged their spoons against their glasses of bug juice.

"Swell," I said to Jed. "The one time there's swimming at night and we can't go in."

Ivan made us sit on the dock. While all the other kids went down the water slide and raced to the raft, we got dive-bombed by mosquitoes. Then all of a sudden there was a crack of lightning. Raindrops seemed to come from nowhere.

The lifeguard blew his whistle. "Everybody out!"

I hate to say it, but we were glad.

More lightning flashed across the sky. The rain was coming down hard now. We were barefoot and the pebbles and pine needles on the ground really made us scramble up the hill. Jed was the last inside our tent.

"Some storm," he said. "I'm soaked."

So were we all. The pink stuff on my face was all soft and runny. What a gross-out! Ivan made

us get into our pj's right away. And when it was time for lights out he said, "I don't want any funny business tonight. You stay in those cots. Do I make myself clear?"

We all nodded. I didn't know about anybody else, but I still itched like crazy. And my head hurt. My cot, even with its scratchy sheets, seemed like a pretty good place to be. The last thing I remember is seeing another crack of lightning.

Then I dreamed I was on a big ship in a storm. The ship was rolling from side to side. I was lying on a bed in a tiny room, wearing a long-sleeved white nightgown. A man was sitting in the room with his back to me.

"Father, Father," I called out. That was weird. I always call my dad Dad. And this guy was definitely not my father.

The guy turned around. It was dark in the room. But I could see that he had a beard. And he was missing an ear!

I bolted up in bed—my real bed in tent 19—with my heart thumping like a tom-tom. Ivan was sitting beside me.

"That was some dream you were having," he

said gently. "You were shouting in your sleep. I had to shake you awake."

Ivan passed me my canteen, which hung from the foot of my cot. I took a gulp of water.

"You okay now?" Ivan asked.

I nodded. "Thanks, Ivan," I said groggily.

Ivan stayed there, sitting beside me, until I was almost asleep. I could feel myself slipping away. I sure hoped I wasn't going to land back in that crazy dream. And I didn't. At least not that night.

# 3.

For the other guys in my tent, life at Tall Pines went back to normal. Our poison ivy got better and nobody thought about ghosts anymore. Nobody but me.

I tried to push that kind of stuff from my mind. But sometimes when I came into the tent, I got hit with a blast of freezing-cold air. It was like opening a refrigerator door. And I kept on having spooky dreams.

Each time I was back on the big ship. I was

always wearing that funny long white night-gown. The scary guy who looked like Captain Blood was always there too. But he didn't act scary in my dreams. He just kept saying stuff like "There, there, laddy. You're sure to be fit again soon."

I didn't tell anybody about the dreams. Not even Jed. But each time Ivan would be there, shaking me awake and calming me down.

I liked Ivan—we all did—even if he was kind of a geek sometimes.

"It was nice of him not to rat on us the night of the camp-out," I said. It was rest period and we were trading baseball cards.

"Yeah," said Jed, who was picking at a scab. "We owe the guy."

So for the next week we really tried to be better campers. It was Arthur's idea. But we all went along with it.

We didn't try to skip any activities. We got good marks in clean-up every day. Hal stopped talking about running away. And he even learned the words to some Tall Pines songs.

One night there was a costume contest in the rec hall. I came up with a good idea. We wrapped ourselves in aluminum foil. We wore nametags that said MINCED HAM, TUNA SURPRISE, VEAL PATTIES, and MYSTERY MEAT.

"We are leftovers from this week's menu," we announced.

Everybody laughed. Cubby too. We won first prize.

"All right!" Ivan said, and punched the air with his fist. "You guys are really shaping up!"

Our prize was a trip into town for ice cream.

We went the next night right after dinner. Ivan took us in Cubby's run-down Jeep to a place called Captain Cone.

The waiters wore pirate hats and plastic swords. The walls were covered with pictures of mean-looking sailors. And the windows were small and round like the windows on a ship.

"So, what's it going to be?" Ivan asked us.

"I'll have the Dead Man's Float with root beer," said Arthur.

Hal and I both ordered Banana Boat Wrecks.

Jed got the biggest thing on the menu. Two people were supposed to share it. It was called the Treasure Chest. It came with six scoops of ice cream and four different sauces.

"Go for it, big fella!" I told Jed.

Arthur shook his head. "You shouldn't egg him on. Do you realize that thing has approximately three thousand calories!"

"Shut up, Arthur," said Jed. At least I think that's what he said. His mouth was so full of ice cream, it was hard to tell.

It took Jed a while to polish off the Treasure Chest. While we waited for him to finish, we read our paper place mats.

At the top of each place mat it said CAPTAIN BLOOD'S TREASURE MAP.

The map showed the town, the bay, a long wiggly line marked POST ROAD, a hill, and way at the top an X between two pine trees.

I turned my place mat over. On the other side was the legend of Captain Blood. It was mostly the same stuff Jed had read to us from that book. Then at the very end it said, "The real map on your place mat was found on a beach by a fisherman long ago. Below the map were written these words: BETWEEN THE TWO TALL PINES I HAVE BURIED MY GREATEST TREASURE. It was signed Henry Bloodworth—in blood!"

All at once I started feeling strange chills again. Maybe it was from eating so much ice cream. But I didn't think so.

"Look at this!" I said. "It's supposed to show

"Shut up, Arthur," said Jed. At least I think that's what he said. His mouth was so full of ice cream, it was hard to tell.

It took Jed a while to polish off the Treasure Chest. While we waited for him to finish, we read our paper place mats.

At the top of each place mat it said CAPTAIN BLOOD'S TREASURE MAP.

The map showed the town, the bay, a long wiggly line marked POST ROAD, a hill, and way at the top an X between two pine trees.

I turned my place mat over. On the other side was the legend of Captain Blood. It was mostly the same stuff Jed had read to us from that book. Then at the very end it said, "The real map on your place mat was found on a beach by a fisherman long ago. Below the map were written these words: BETWEEN THE TWO TALL PINES I HAVE BURIED MY GREATEST TREASURE. It was signed Henry Bloodworth—in blood!"

All at once I started feeling strange chills again. Maybe it was from eating so much ice cream. But I didn't think so.

"Look at this!" I said. "It's supposed to show

where Captain Blood hid his treasure."

Jed stopped eating and let out a sonic boom of a burp.

"Wow!" he said. "A real treasure map!"

"Dream on," Arthur said flatly. "If this map was real, the treasure would have been found already."

"You know," said Hal, "this map looks kind of like the map—" Then he shut up fast.

"Like what map?" Ivan asked as he paid the check.

Hal sounded flustered. "Oh, um. Like a map I once saw in a book."

As Ivan led us out of Captain Cone I saw Hal

grab his place mat and stick it in his pocket.

"I've got something to show you," Hal whispered to us when we were back in the Jeep. "But I don't want Ivan to see."

"Wait until he's asleep," I whispered back. "We can talk then."

We all pretended to go to sleep right away. As soon as we heard Ivan snoring those big, log-sawing snores of his we tiptoed over to Hal's cot.

Hal looked really excited. He turned on his flashlight and showed us two pieces of paper. One was the place mat from Captain Cone. The other was the map he had drawn at the infirmary—his running-away map.

"You're not going to believe this," Hal said. "Look!" He pointed to the X on Captain Blood's map. It was at the top of the hill between two pine trees. Then he pointed to the little square on his map that was for tent 19. The little square was at the top of the hill between the two tree stumps.

"So?" said Jed. Sometimes Jed can really be dense.

"Jed, don't you see?" I had a hard time keeping my voice down. "The X on the treasure map is right where our tent is!"

"It looks like Hal really might be on to something," Arthur said a little grudgingly. I guess Arthur figured that he's such a brain he should have been the one to put two and two together.

"I know I'm right," Hal said importantly. "It says it here." Hal began reading from the back of the place mat. " 'Between the two tall pines I have buried my greatest treasure.' Well, that's where our tent is—between two tall pines. Only they aren't tall pines anymore. Now they're just tree stumps."

"We're going to be rich! We're going to be rich!" Jed said over and over. The beam from Hal's flashlight was shining on Jed's round face. I swear you could practically see little dollar signs in his eyes.

"Now all we need is a plan for digging up the treasure," Arthur said, scratching an ear thoughtfully.

And of course he came up with a beaut!

# 4.

Arthur's plan was put into action the next day.

Step one was to "borrow" three big serving spoons from the mess hall.

"Since we don't have any shovels, we have to use the spoons for digging," Arthur explained to us.

Step two was to wait for Ivan's night out. That wasn't for three days.

"Bye, Ivan!" We waved as Ivan crunched up the gravel path and out the main entrance.

"Have a great time. Don't hurry back!"

After the lights-out bell, we waited for about half an hour. Then we drew straws to see who was going to be lookout. And sure enough, I got stuck with the short straw.

"Remember to call out if you see anyone coming," Arthur said as he and Jed and Hal crawled under the tent.

I went and sat on the tree stump to the left of the tent. From where I sat I could see the whole camp. If a counselor decided to check up on us, I would have enough time to warn the others. I was wearing a dark blue sweatshirt so that I blended in with the shadows.

"How's it going?" I called softly after about ten minutes.

"We've already dug down about a foot," Jed whispered back. "But all we've found are some old soda cans."

"Hey, no more talking," Arthur hissed out. "We have work to do."

I sat there in the dark for a while. It was a peaceful night. And the pine trees all around camp made the air smell nice . . . like at Christmas. The only noise I could hear was a radio from the counselors' shack by the bay.

Then all at once I felt a chill. The hair on the back of my neck started tingling and I began to shiver. I pulled my legs up to my chest and wrapped my arms around them. But I couldn't get warm.

Suddenly there was a rush of air that made the flaps on our tent move in and out. It looked almost like the tent was breathing! And I heard someone crying. It must be some homesick kid, I told myself. Or someone having a bad dream. I wished I believed it. The creepy feeling was coming over me. Stronger than ever.

The crying got a little louder. And then I saw him.

At first there was just a misty white blob. It

floated between the tent and me. I blinked my eyes and stared. And as I watched, the blob took on color and shape. An outline appeared. It got clearer and sharper. Like somebody tuning in a TV set.

It was a boy. He was about my age. He was dressed in a long white nightshirt and his hair was pulled back in a pigtail. His eyes looked puffy and swollen as if he'd been crying for a real long time.

"I'm not seeing this," I said out loud. My teeth were chattering like crazy. And it wasn't just 'cause I was scared stiff. It was so cold now that when I breathed out, it showed, like little puffs of smoke!

"Please help me," the ghost boy said. He sounded sad. And he had a funny way of talking so it came out sounding like "Ploise elp me."

"What—what do you want?" I managed to croak out. It was weird. I could hear the guys just a few feet away from me under the tent. But it felt like there was nobody else in the whole world right now except for me and the ghost boy.

"I want to go home. I want me dad." The ghost boy's hand reached out to me. But I shrank

back. "Help me," he said again softly. And then, right before my eyes, he started to get all transparent. In a few seconds I could see the tent clear through him. I blinked and when my eyes opened, he was gone. Gone completely.

Then I heard my own voice.

"Jed! Jed!" I cried. "Come quick!"

Jed, Arthur, and Hal came scrambling out from under the tent. "What is it?" Jed raced over to the tree stump where I was still sitting and shook me. "Is somebody coming?"

"Somebody did come." I tried to breathe deeply. My heart was jumping around all over the place. And I didn't trust myself to stand up. "But you aren't going to believe it."

The guys saw I was in bad shape and they helped me back to the tent. Then I told them everything. I told them about seeing the ghost boy and what he said. I told them about my spooky dreams, too.

"Captain Blood is in every dream with me," I said. "Only now I don't think it's really me in the dreams. I think it's the ghost boy."

I looked up at Jed and Hal and Arthur. I could

tell from their white faces and scared eyes that they believed me.

Hal gulped. "Oh, gosh! What if there's a curse on the tent?" He gulped again. "I saw this movie once. A ghost was living in a deserted house. Then this family moves in and they start to fix up the house. Only the ghost doesn't like that. So one by one the ghost kills off the family. It all seems like accidents. But it's really the ghost!" Hal's voice broke. He was really worked up now. "I don't know about you guys. But I'm getting out of this place. Tomorrow I'm calling my parents. And if they won't come and get me, I really will run away."

"Hold on, Hal," I said. "This is very scary stuff, for sure. You don't have to tell me that. I mean, I'm the one who saw the ghost and everything. But I don't think this ghost is out to get us. Really I don't. He doesn't look mean. He looks sad. He just wants his father."

"Oh, boy. I hope you're right, Danny," Jed said. "This whole thing gives me major creeps. I say we forget about the treasure hunt right now."

*Incredible!* I thought. *Jed must really be scared if*

*he's talking about giving up on the treasure!*

"Jed's right," Arthur said. "Ghosts don't like to be disturbed. They like to be left in peace. No more digging."

We all nodded and locked pinkies on it.

Then the four of us froze. All at once cold air was rippling through our tent. And we heard a voice—a boy's voice near the door—say softly but very clearly, "Please keep on digging."

# 5.

Let me tell you, nobody got any sleep that night. After we heard the voice, we all screamed and grabbed each other. Hal's eyes rolled back behind his thick glasses and he fainted dead away. We had to slap him and throw water in his face before he came to.

By the next morning we were all a little calmer. Not much, but a little. At softball, while we were waiting to be up at bat, we talked about what had happened. We figured it this way: If a

CAMP
TALL
PINES

ghost tells you to do something, you do it. Period.

So on Ivan's next night out we went digging again. This time Hal was lookout. Arthur, Jed, and I burrowed under the tent.

"The more I think about it," I said to Jed and Arthur, "the more sure I am that the ghost boy wants us to find the treasure. And tonight is the night. I feel it in my bones."

"There's our hole," Jed whispered, pointing at it with his flashlight. "I sure hope we're digging in the right spot."

The hole was nice and deep. But the minute I saw it, I knew we were way off base. Don't ask me how I knew. I just knew. So I started crawling around in the dark, looking for a better spot. As I moved toward the center of the tent, it felt like a magnet was pulling me. It got colder and colder. By the time I reached a spot that was just about dead center under our tent, I felt like I was at the North Pole. This was the spot all right!

I started digging. Almost right away my spoon hit something hard.

"Jed. Arthur. Over here," I called softly. "I think I found something."

Jed and Arthur were there in a flash. Hal too.

"This is it!" Jed crooned. "Fame and fortune! I bet we'll be on the cover of *People* magazine!"

I grabbed a flashlight from Hal and clicked it on. The beam of light was shining down on a flat, smooth stone. I brushed away some dirt. The stone was about two feet wide and there seemed to be letters carved on it.

"Guess what, guys. This is no treasure chest," Arthur said.

I brushed away more dirt. I could make out some writing now.

" 'John Bloodworth,' " I read off slowly. " 'Rest in peace.' "

"Oh, no! This is a grave!" Jed cried out. "Captain Blood's grave!"

"I'm out of here," said Hal. He started to crawl out. But Arthur held on to the end of his T-shirt.

"Not so fast," Arthur said. "This can't be Captain Blood's grave. He died at sea. And anyway, his first name was Henry, not John. I remember that from the treasure map."

Hal looked like he might pass out again. But he stayed where he was.

I brushed off the rest of the stone. Now it read:

JOHN BLOODWORTH

REST IN PEACE

1707–1716

It was as if the pieces of a puzzle suddenly all flew into place. Now I understood. I under-

stood all my strange dreams. And I understood what we had just found.

"Gosh," said Jed. "John Bloodworth was just a kid when he died. Do you think he was killed and put here to guard the treasure?"

I shook my head and pointed to the gravestone.

"This *is* the treasure," I said.

Jed looked blank. So did Hal. But Arthur snapped his fingers. "Oh! I get it now!"

"Remember what Captain Blood wrote on his treasure map?" I said to Jed and Hal. " 'Between the two tall pines I have buried my greatest treasure.' Well, he wasn't talking about gold or jewels. He was talking about John Bloodworth. John Bloodworth was his son. And John Bloodworth is the ghost boy!"

# 6.

A little while later we snuck back into our tent. We all sat huddled together on the bare wood floor. Jed pulled out a couple of stale Snickers bars he'd hidden in his laundry bag.

"So what do we do now?" he asked, passing a piece to each of us.

"Do you think we should tell Ivan?" Hal asked, looking over in the direction of Ivan's empty cot.

"I just don't know," I said. I licked some

chocolate from my fingers. "Maybe the ghost boy wouldn't want us to."

Later that night I found out.

I was almost asleep when I started feeling cold all over. I scrunched down under my army blanket. Forget it. That didn't help at all.

"Danny! Danny!" a voice with a funny accent called softly. I had heard that voice before.

I sat up fast.

At the end of my cot, by the screen window of the tent, was a misty white light. As I watched, the light took shape and in a few seconds there was the ghost boy. In living color. I was plenty scared. I'd be lying if I said I wasn't. But I wasn't scared like the time before. It didn't even surprise me that the ghost boy knew my name.

"You're John, aren't you?" I asked him. "Captain Blood's son."

"Ay. That I am," said the ghost boy. His voice was high and kind of sweet. "We were bound for Nova Scotia, me dad and me, when I fell sick. I knew it was bad. And not more'n a fortnight later I was laid to rest here. But before I died, me dad swore by the Jolly Roger that one day he would come back for me . . . and he will."

The ghost boy stood there in his nightgown, staring at me with those sad, teary eyes of his as if he was daring me to say different.

"Do you know that your father died soon after you?" I asked softly. "His ship sank in a storm at sea." I felt bad saying this to him. "Maybe he can't get back to you."

The ghost boy shook his head. "His spirit will return for me," he said calmly. "I know it."

I shrugged. "Maybe so," I said. I didn't want to hurt his feelings. But I figured if his father hadn't showed up by now, he wasn't ever coming.

Then it hit me. And I felt dumb for not thinking of it before.

"Say! Maybe your dad is having trouble finding you. I mean, he buried you between two tall pines. But those trees are gone now! And our tent is right over your grave. I bet if we got the tent moved, your dad *could* find you."

The ghost boy seemed almost to smile now. Then he started to get all shimmery around the edges and the color drained right out of him so that he looked like a large boy-shaped cloud.

The cloud drifted apart and grew paler until it was completely gone.

I sat there on my cot, looking for some trace of him. But all I heard was a soft whisper: "Thanks, mate!"

# 7.

A lot of things happened the next day.

First I told the guys about talking to John. Then we went and told Ivan about looking for treasure and finding the grave instead. We didn't lie to him. We just left out all the ghost stuff.

Ivan's eyes popped. He was so excited that when he spoke, little bits of spit flew into his beard. "Captain Blood's son! Outrageous! We'd better go up and see the big guy about this. We'd better go right now!" Ivan was already out of the tent, heading for Cubby's office.

"Well, well. So you've found the grave of a pirate's son" was all Cubby had to say to us. "Now, that sure is something you'll always remember from your days at Tall Pines."

Cubby was sitting behind an old metal desk in his office off the mess hall. There was a huge pile of bills in front of him. Right away he went back to paying them. It was pretty clear he wanted us to beat it.

"But what about the tent?" I asked in a louder voice than I meant to. "You have to move it."

Cubby looked up over the rims of his glasses.

"I don't see why," he said flatly. "That's an unnecessary expense. The tent's been there for years. And John Bloodworth has never complained about the noise."

Cubby had a good chuckle over that one. I was getting mad. "But if the tent stays where it is, he won't—"

Arthur jabbed me in the side.

"Who won't? What are you talking about?" asked Cubby.

"Uh—Danny's talking about the reporter

CAMP
TALL
PINES
CAMP
TALL
PINES
CAMP
TALL
PINES
CAMP
TALL
PINES
CAMP
TALL
PINES

from the *Manchester Herald,*" Arthur said real fast. "I hope you don't mind but I called the paper already. They think it's a great human interest story . . . and it'll be good publicity for the camp too."

*Way to go, Arthur,* I thought.

That turned Cubby around very fast. Of course, what Arthur said wasn't exactly true. But later we got Ivan to call the local paper and they really did want to see the gravestone.

The story and our picture appeared a few days later. In the story we were called "four spunky lads," which made us sound like total dips. And they said my name was Donny. Still, we were the stars of camp for a while. And the tent did get moved to the other side of the main path.

After that the rest of the summer was pretty quiet. Hal found hair in his spaghetti and talked about suing Cubby. Arthur won the camp chess tournament. Jed went on a diet—for a day.

As for me, I didn't see John Bloodworth again. I stopped having dreams about him too. But that didn't mean I stopped thinking about him.

Then, before we knew it, it was the last night

of camp. We stayed up late, packing all our junk and remembering the dumb stuff that had happened that summer.

After a while we got quiet. We knew we wouldn't be seeing each other for an awfully long time. I put my autograph book in my suitcase and some Polaroid pictures I'd taken of Ivan and the guys. I squeezed my suitcase shut. The summer really was ending.

I stood up. "I don't know about you guys," I said. "But I'm going outside to say good-bye."

The others knew exactly what I was talking about. They followed me out of the tent.

We walked over to the gravestone and stood around it for a couple of minutes. It was a foggy night, so you couldn't see any of the other tents. It felt like we were all alone on top of the hill.

"I hope you see your dad real soon," I said silently to John.

Then in the distance a bell started ringing slowly.

"What's that?" asked Hal nervously.

"It's not the camp bell," said Jed. "I know that."

The sound of the bell grew a little louder. We

turned toward the bay, where the ringing was coming from. The fog began to part. Then we saw it. Not just me. We *all* saw it.

It was a ship, big and black, with about a hundred sails on it. Long rope ladders hung from the mast like giant spider webs. And cannons poked out from each side of the ship. It was the ship's bell that was ringing.

Jed cupped his hands over his eyes and squinted down at the bay. "Will you get a load of that!" he said in a hoarse whisper.

The ship sailed closer and closer. But it didn't make a single ripple in the water. Now I could see a flag—a flag with a skull and bones on it—flapping from the mast.

"It's—it's Captain Blood's ship, isn't it?" Hal stuttered.

Arthur nodded and made a sound like a tiny squeal.

Then suddenly a rush of air whooshed past us. And for a second, just a split second, I saw John. He was still wearing that long nightgown. His arms were stretched out wide and he was running. Well, not running exactly. He seemed to float down the hill and across the water to the ship.

"John's going home too!" I cried.

A minute later the ship turned around and began to sail away. We waved like mad. I wasn't sure, but I thought I saw two figures standing on the deck, waving back at us. Then the fog closed in again and the ship was gone forever.

We stood there for a little bit. But there was nothing more to see. So we trooped back to the tent.

That night, when I fell asleep, I had a wonderful dream. I dreamed about a big ship. There was a strong wind and the sky was bright blue. The air was soft and warm. A tall man with a

black beard stood beside a young boy. His arm was around the boy's shoulder. And I knew John was home at last!

## About the Authors

"I've always liked ghost stories," says JIM O'CONNOR. "What I liked most about writing this story was making the treasure an unusual one. It's not gold or silver; it's something far more precious—even to a pirate."

JANE O'CONNOR says, "We wanted *The Ghost in Tent 19* to be spooky *and* funny—I hope it is!"

Jim and Jane O'Connor live in New York City with their two young sons.

## About the Illustrator

CHARLES ROBINSON has illustrated dozens of children's books, including *Soup on Ice, Soup's Goat,* and *Soup in the Saddle,* by Robert Newton Peck. "I really enjoyed illustrating *The Ghost in Tent 19,*" he says. "It reminded me of my own days as a camper, although I never met a ghost at *my* camp."

Charles Robinson lives with his wife in Mendham, New Jersey.